EASTER EGG HAUNT

written by Mike Thaler
illustrated by Jared Lee

 ZONDERkidz

ZONDERVAN.com/
AUTHORTRACKER
follow your favorite authors

To Annette
—M.T.

To Carolyn Lee
—J.L.

ZONDER**kidz**™

Easter Egg Haunt
Copyright © 2009 by Mike Thaler
Illustrations © 2009 by Jared Lee Studio, Inc.

Requests for information should be addressed to:
Zonderkidz, *Grand Rapids, Michigan 49530*

Library of Congress Cataloging-in-Publication Data: Applied for ISBN 978-0-310-71591-7

Thaler, Mike, 1936-
    Easter egg haunt / by Mike Thaler ; illustrated by Jared Lee.
        p. cm. -- (Tales from the back pew)
    Summary: A young boy and his Sunday school classmates learn about the true spirit of Easter while decorating eggs for the church Easter egg hunt.
        ISBN 978-0-310-71591-7 (softcover) [1. Easter--Fiction. 2. Easter eggs--Fiction. 3. Christian life--Fiction. 4. Humorous stories.] I. Lee, Jared D., ill. II. Title.
PZ7.T3Eas 2009
[E]--dc22
                                                                              2008007596

Editor: Betsy Flikkema
Art Director: Merit Alderink

Printed in China

09 10 11 12 • 5 4 3 2 1

It's Easter, and our church is going to have an Easter egg hunt.
I hope they're not scrambled!

I wonder if our preacher is going to dress up like a giant bunny, Bunzilla or the Easter Mummy.

PREACHER
CREATURE →

In Sunday school class we decorated the eggs. All the girls painted flowers.

The boys painted clowns.

GIANT CHICK

HA, HA, HA.

I painted Frankenstein.

← HARRYSTEIN

SALLYSTEIN →

My Sunday school teacher said it wasn't quite the spirit of Easter.
I asked him, "What is the spirit of Easter?" He said Easter is about
love and life. Then he sat us down and told us a story.

After Jesus died on the cross, He was buried in a cave behind a big rock that was guarded by Roman soldiers.

CHICKEN

PARROT

CROW

DOVE

OWL

It was Friday, and His friends missed Him very much.

They didn't believe Him when He said, "I'll be back in three days." They had forgotten that God is a God of miracles and always keeps His word.

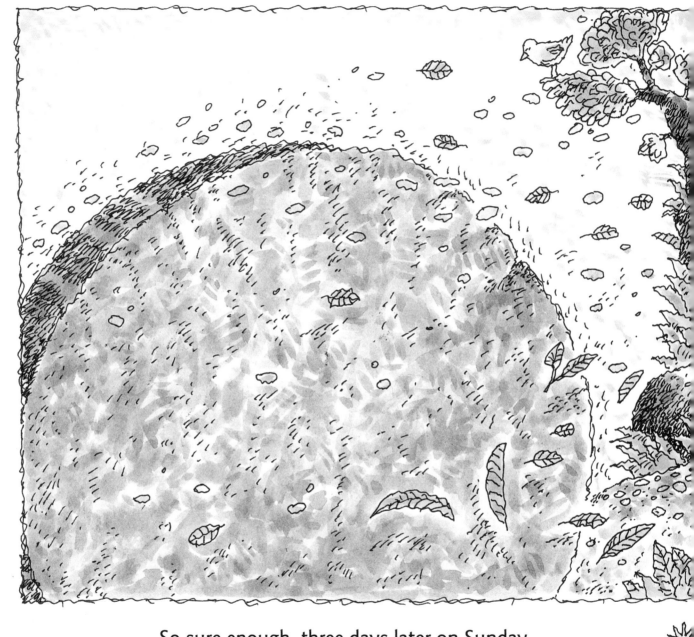

So sure enough, three days later on Sunday,
the rock rolled away and Jesus came back.

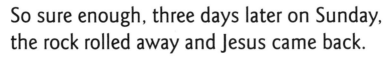

"Was that the beginning of ROCK AND ROLL?" I asked.
"No, but it was the beginning of new life for us all."

Jesus said He loves us very much and will always be with us.
And one day, He'll take us to live with Him in heaven.

"Why is it called Easter and not Wester?" I asked. My teacher scratched his head. "I'm not sure," he said. "Maybe it's because the Son rises in the east," I exclaimed. "Maybe." My teacher smiled. "Maybe."

 "And what's that got to do with eggs?" I asked.
"Well," answered my teacher, "the eggs are eggstra.

"People added them to the holiday …
sort of like Santa Claus was added to Christmas."

JELLYBEAN

ROCK

"And what about the Easter Bunny?"
"He hopped aboard too."

"So," I said, "Easter is really all about Jesus."
"Like everything else." My teacher smiled. "Like everything else."

For God so loved the world that
he gave his one and only Son, that
whoever believes in him shall not
perish but have eternal life.

—John 3:16